THE BEAR WHO WASN'T THERE

OREN LAVIE

THE BEAR WHO WASN'T THERE

AND THE FABULOUS FOREST

ILLUSTRATIONS BY WOLF ERLBRUCH

Once upon a Time there was an Itch.

Simply, an Itch.

It wasn't a very big Itch.
It wasn't a small Itch, either.
It was a medium-size Itch.
And the Itch wanted to scratch.

Once upon a Time.

Sometime later, at about quarter past Once upon a Time, the Itch wandered by a tree and started to scratch against it. Now a very strange thing happened: the Itch began to grow in size. In fact, the more it scratched the bigger it grew.

That's funny, thought the Itch and kept scratching.

A minute later fur began to cover the Itch, and the fur grew arms and legs and a nose, and before long the Itch looked very much like . . . a bear.

A BEAR????

Well, everybody knows that bears scratch when they itch, but not many people know that itches scratch when they're *bears!*

And indeed, the more the Itch scratched the more it was a bear, until finally in the place where there was no bear before now stood **The Bear Who Wasn't There**!

The Bear opened his eyes and smiled.
"Absolutely yes!" he said, because he was a very positive bear.
He looked to his left and to his right and discovered that he was all alone.
Am I the first? he thought. *Am I the last?* And he wondered whether it was better to be first or last when you were all alone.

Next, he discovered he had a pocket.

He slipped his hand into the pocket
and found a folded piece of paper. It said:

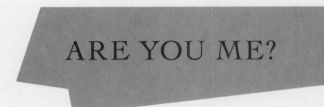

ARE YOU ME?

The Bear scratched his head. "A very good question."

He continued to read.

ARE YOU ME?
HELPFUL CLUES TO LOOK FOR:
1. I AM A VERY NICE BEAR
2. I AM A HAPPY BEAR
3. VERY HANDSOME TOO

"Oh good," said the Bear, "I hope I *am* me."
And he began to walk.

A Fabulous Forest was now growing all around the Bear wherever he looked, and the Bear could not help but wonder whether the forest would still grow if he wasn't looking, so he closed his eyes. But then he couldn't really tell. So he peeked . . .

The forest was still growing! And the Bear thought:

THE MORE I LOOK
THE LESS I KNOW
IF TREES AND FLOWERS GROW
WHEN I'M NOT LOOKING.

It was a beautiful thought, and the Bear wrote it down with a pencil that he found behind his ear.

The Fabulous Forest was very quiet that time of Once upon a Time, and the Bear could hear different types of silence. There was the small silence of the leaves, and the deep silence of the ground, and the old silence of the trees. There was one silence which was the most silent of all and the hardest one to spot: it was his own silence. The Bear listened carefully and followed the sound of his own silence, which took him into the heart of the forest.

Suddenly he saw a peculiar figure in the distance.
It was waving at him.

The peculiar figure turned out to be not one but *two* peculiar figures sitting one on top of the other. They were the **Convenience Cow** and the **Lazy Lizard**.

The Convenience Cow was a large, soft cow in the shape of a sofa. You could also say that she was a large, soft sofa with the personality of a cow. She was an easy cow to get along with. She was also an easy sofa to get along with.

The Lazy Lizard was a skinny creature, dressed in a crumpled suit. He was sitting lazily, as he always did, on the back of the Convenience Cow, puffing his big cigar. He was too lazy to walk by himself. He was too lazy to stand by himself. He was too lazy to sit by himself. Sometimes he managed to fall by himself, but only very short distances.

"Hello," said the Bear.

"Hello, Bear," said the Cow, "good to
see you."

"Do you *know* me?" the Bear asked.

"Of course I do," the Cow smiled.

The Bear scratched his head.

"Do I know . . . *you*?"

"You most certainly do," the
Cow said.

"Are we *friends*?" The Bear had high hopes.

"Of course we are," the Cow smiled.

"Really?" The Bear clapped his hands and turned to the Lazy Lizard. "Are we friends too?"

The Lizard took a big puff from his cigar and, after a long pause, said, "Very old friends."

This was good news. Making new friends was good, but making *old* friends was much better.

"Please be honest," the Bear lowered his voice and leaned forward, "do you happen to know if I'm a *nice* bear?"

"The nicest bear I've ever met," said the Cow.

The Bear blushed. "I had a feeling," he said.

He fished out the piece of paper from his pocket and marked:

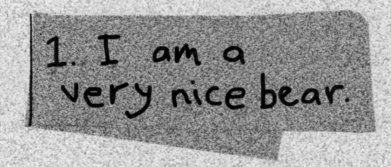

"And now I must run," the Bear said.

"Where are you going?" asked the Cow.

"To find out if I am really me."

"I hope you are," said the Cow.

The Bear was walking and whistling, whistling and walking, through the forest. Sometimes he whistled faster than he walked and sometimes he walked louder than he whistled, but most of the time he walked and whistled exactly the same because it was the best way.

When the whistling came to an end the Bear found himself standing next to a funny-looking creature. It was the **Penultimate Penguin**.

The Penultimate Penguin was a short, chubby character. He was standing under a tall tree, gazing at his own shadow with a thoughtful expression on his face.

"Hello," said the Bear.

"Shhhh . . ." whispered the Penultimate Penguin.

"I am a bear," the Bear whispered back.

"Sshhhhh," whispered the Penultimate Penguin.

"A *nice* bear," the Bear winked, "I am told."

"I can't talk right now," said the Penguin. "I am busy."

"What are you doing?"

"Thinking."

"Can I think with you?"

"As long as you don't think about the same thing."

"Okay . . . what are you thinking about?"

"Everything!"

The Bear scratched his head. "Could you maybe leave a little something for *me* to think about?"

"Absolutely not!" said the Penguin. "For a brain as large as mine, Everything is barely enough. Sometimes I have no choice but to think about Everything *twice*."

"But then what would that leave *me* to think about?" asked the Bear.

"Nothing!" said the Penguin.

"Wonderful, I'll think about Nothing, then," the Bear said happily.

"Impossible!" cried the Penguin. "I am thinking about that too."

"But you're thinking about Everything," the Bear said.

"Nothing is part of Everything."

"Oh well, never mind," said the Bear. "I'll just smell the flowers."

"The flowers?" The Penguin raised an eyebrow. "I've already counted the flowers twice this morning."

"I wonder if I can count," the Bear mused.

"I won't be surprised if you can't," said the Penguin.

"Me neither," the Bear said cheerfully, then began to count:

"One flower . . .
　　two flowers . . .
red flowers . . .
　　　blue flowers . . .
　　　　　tall flowers . . .
　　and . . .
　　　Beautiful flowers!"

And he concluded: "There are exactly Beautiful flowers around the tree."

The Penultimate Penguin looked at him narrowly and said, "Beautiful is not a number."

"Oh, but I just counted," said the Bear.

"And that was not *counting*."

"No?" said the Bear.

"Not even close," said the Penguin. "Now let me tell you: the number of flowers around that tree is exactly thirty-eight. Remember that!"

"Beautiful is easier to remember," said the Bear.

"Beautiful is *not* a number!"

"Beautiful may not be a *regular* number," the Bear explained, "but it's a *special* number for flowers."

"No it's not!" the Penguin shrieked.

But the Bear was no longer paying attention; his nose was deep inside the flower bed, sniffing the flowers. The smell of flowers made his nose tickle and he laughed.

"I must go," he said cheerfully. "Goodbye."

He walked away thinking to himself:

Better to smell flowers than to count them.

And he thought:

Flowers are more Beautiful than they are thirty-eight.

The thought made him very happy. He wrote on his piece of paper:

2. I am a happy bear

Next the Bear came to a large tree. It was the Compass Tree.

The Fabulous Forest had not four but eight directions: East, West, South, North, Wrong, Right, Lunch, and Breakfast.

Presently the Bear was debating whether it was going to be Lunch or Breakfast for him, when he heard a voice.

"Anybody call a taxi?"

From behind the tree appeared a **Turtle Taxi**.

"Not me," said the Bear.

"Are you sure?" The Turtle looked disappointed.

"I just got here," said the Bear.

"Where did you come from?" the Turtle asked.

"Well," the Bear scratched his head thoughtfully, "I came from *Behind* me."

"That's strange," the Turtle said. "I was just there and didn't see you."

"I must have just left," the Bear explained.

"And where are you going?" asked the Turtle.

"It seems to me," the Bear said, "that I am going *Forward*."

The Turtle nodded. "Yes, I know the place. It's very popular. Everybody seems to be going there nowadays."

"Do they?" the Bear said excitedly. "Is it far?"

"Sometimes it is," the Turtle shrugged, "sometimes it isn't." He began to chew a small leaf, trying to remember which time it was and which time it wasn't. "It really depends on who's going."

"*I'm* going," said the Bear.

"Of course, you could always consider calling a taxi," the Turtle suggested helpfully.

"Taxi!!" the Bear called out.

The Turtle Taxi disappeared behind the tree, then came out on the other side.

"Anybody call a taxi?"

"I did!"

And so the two began moving Forward. Very slowly.

"Slowly," said the Turtle, "is the only way to get anywhere in this forest."

After some time had passed the Bear asked, "Are we lost?"

"Yes we are," the Turtle nodded. "It's part of the way Forward."

"I see," said the Bear.

And sometime later the Bear asked, "Are we still lost?"

"Absolutely," replied the Turtle.

"Oh good," said the Bear.

Then the Turtle stopped, smelled one of the trees, chewed a small bush, and declared, "Just as I thought, we've arrived. This is Forward."

"Oh boy!" the Bear said.

"Good luck," said the Turtle.

"Drive carefully," said the Bear.

The Bear arrived at the front gate of a house.
I wonder who lives here, he thought. A sign on the door said:

HOME OF THE BEAR WHO WASN'T THERE
(please enter quietly, he may be asleep)

"Oh, I see," said the Bear, "*I* live here!"
And he entered the house quietly,
careful not to wake himself up.

"What a Beautiful house I have," he said. "Who knew?!"

The entire house was built around a wonderful Scratching Tree and the furniture was placed in a circle surrounding it. There was a large mirror hanging from the tree.

The Bear looked at himself in the mirror and smiled.
The Bear in the mirror was no doubt a *very handsome* bear.
"Nice to meet me," he said.
"Nice to meet me too," he answered politely.
"I had a feeling I might be me," he said. "I felt familiar."
"Me too," he answered.

And he wrote:

SOME BEARS LOOK EXACTLY LIKE THEMSELVES
WHEN THEY LOOK INTO THE MIRROR (AND WINK)
AND THAT'S HOW I RECOGNIZED MYSELF (I THINK!)

1. I am a very nice bear.
2. I am a happy bear.
3. I am a <u>very</u> <u>handsome</u> bear.

Oren Lavie has green eyes, long curly hair, and relatively cold feet. He was born in June, one week behind schedule, and has been trying to catch up ever since. He likes to sleep late but does his best writing early in the morning, which is why his best writing so rarely gets done. Oren is a musician, director, and author of children's books. His debut album, *The Opposite Side of the Sea*, was released worldwide to critical acclaim, winning him the prestigious ASCAP Foundation Sammy Cahn Award for his lyrics. The music video for "Her Morning Elegance" was nominated for a Grammy Award and became a YouTube hit. Oren wrote "A Dance 'Round the Memory Tree" for *The Chronicles of Narnia: Prince Caspian* movie. *The Bear Who Wasn't There* is his first book to be published in the US.

Wolf Erlbruch is one of Germany's most renowned illustrators; his work is respected and loved around the world. Among his many awards, Wolf has received both the Gutenberg and the German Children's Literature Award, as well as a Hans Christian Andersen Illustrator Award. His previous book, *Duck, Death and the Tulip*, sold more than 100,000 copies and was published in nineteen countries.

Words ©2014, 2016 Oren Lavie
Illustrations ©2014, 2016 Wolf Erlbruch
Edited by Yael Ornan
Originally published in 2014 in Germany by Verlag Antje Kunstmann GmbH

ISBN: 978-1-61775-490-6
Library of Congress Control Number: 2016935178
First printing

Black Sheep/Akashic Books
Twitter: @AkashicBooks
Facebook: AkashicBooks
E-mail: info@akashicbooks.com
Website: www.akashicbooks.com

Printed in China by Four Colour Print Group, Louisville, Kentucky
Production Date: May 2016
Batch Number: 66738-0
Plant Location: Guangdong, China